TO THE PETTY, HEUER, AND
DALTON FAMILIES

PRESENTS

THE AMERICAN GIRLS COLLECTION®

18 54

19 04

19 44

CHANGES FOR
SAMANTHA
A WINTER STORY

BY VALERIE TRIPP

ILLUSTRATIONS LUANN ROBERTS

SCHOLASTIC INC.
NEW YORK TORONTO LONDON AUCKLAND SYDNEY

PICTURE CREDITS

The following individuals and organizations have generously given permission to reprint illustrations contained in "Looking Back:" pp. 62-63—Culver Pictures; Brown Brothers; Brown Brothers; State Historical Society of Wisconsin; The Bettmann Archive; pp. 64-65—Mrs. Lora Timmy; C.J. Hibbard, Minnesota Historical Society; State Historical Society of Wisconsin; Jane Addams Memorial Collection, Special Collections, The University Library, University of Illinois at Chicago; Jane Addams Memorial Collection, Special Collections, The University Library, University of Illinois at Chicago; State Historical Society of Wisconsin; pp. 66-67—State Historical Society of Wisconsin; Cincinatti Art Museum, Purchase; gift of Mrs. J. Louis Ransohoff, by exchange; Culver Pictures; Reprinted with permission of Butterick Company, Inc., 161 Avenue of the Americas, New York, NY 10013.

Edited by Jeanne Thieme
Designed by Myland McRevey
Art Directed by Kathleen A. Brown

ISBN 0-590-45082-4

Copyright © 1988 by Pleasant Company.
All rights reserved. Published by Scholastic Inc.,
730 Broadway, New York, NY 10003, by arrangement
with Pleasant Company.

12 11 10 9   4 5 6 7/9

Printed in the U.S.A.   23

First Scholastic printing, March 1992

TABLE OF CONTENTS

SAMANTHA'S FAMILY

GRANDMARY
Samantha's grandmother, who is living on a yacht with her husband the Admiral.

ADMIRAL ARCHIBALD BEEMIS
The jolly Englishman who married Grandmary and became a great grandfather.

SAMANTHA
A wealthy orphan who moves to New York City to live with her aunt and uncle.

UNCLE GARD
Samantha's favorite uncle, who calls her Sam.

AUNT CORNELIA
An old-fashioned beauty who has new-fangled ideas.

NELLIE
Samantha's poor friend,
who works
as a maid.

AGNES & AGATHA
Samantha's newest
friends, who are
Cornelia's sisters.

JESSIE
Grandmary's
seamstress, who
"patches
Samantha up."

HAWKINS
Grandmary's butler
and driver.

MRS. HAWKINS
The cook at
Grandmary's house
in Mount Bedford.

CHAPTER ONE

A NEW HOME

Samantha hurried along the city sidewalk with her ice skates slung over one shoulder. Oh, it was cold! She pulled her hat down over her ears and then rubbed her hands together inside her snug fur muff. The wintry afternoon sky was pink darkening to purple as she ran up the steps to Uncle Gard and Aunt Cornelia's house. "Hello!" she called out as she pushed open the heavy door and came into the bright hallway. "I'm home!"

"There you are, dear!" said Aunt Cornelia. She gave Samantha a hug. "I was afraid you'd frozen to the ice! It must have been awfully cold at the skating pond this afternoon. Come sit by the fire and have some tea. That will warm you up."

Samantha followed Aunt Cornelia into the cozy parlor. She sat by the fire and held her stiff hands up to the glow to melt the coldness away. This was Samantha's favorite time of the day now that she lived in New York City with Uncle Gard and Aunt Cornelia. Every afternoon as dusk settled over the city, Samantha and Aunt Cornelia shared a pot of tea and chatted while they waited for Uncle Gard to come home from his office. This afternoon, Samantha noticed a big box on the tea table. A bit of silky pink ribbon was slipping out from under the lid. "What's in the box, Aunt Cornelia?" she asked.

"Valentines!" said Aunt Cornelia. She lifted the lid and turned the box upside-down. Out spilled loops of ribbon, paper lace doilies, tiny red hearts, and sheets of paper covered with pictures of cupids and flowers. "Saint Valentine's Day is only a few weeks away. I thought we'd better start making our valentines now, since—"

"We have so many to make this year!" Samantha finished eagerly. She picked up a pink ribbon and two hearts. "My first valentine will be for Grandmary and the Admiral."

"The newly-weds!" smiled Aunt Cornelia.

"I'll make two hearts joined together," said Samantha. "That seems right for people who just got married, doesn't it?"

"Yes, indeed!" said Aunt Cornelia. She began cutting out pictures of cupids.

"Oh, it's so romantic," sighed Samantha. "I mean the way Grandmary and the Admiral finally got married after being so fond of each other for all those years."

"Mmm," agreed Aunt Cornelia.

"I'm sure they're happy, sailing around the world on the Admiral's yacht," said Samantha. "I do miss them both just terribly. But I'm glad I live here with you and Uncle Gard."

"We're glad, too!" smiled Aunt Cornelia.

Just then the parlor door opened. "Begging your pardon, Madam," a cool voice interrupted. It was Gertrude, the housekeeper. She was carrying the tea tray. Samantha sat up a little straighter. Gertrude always made her feel as if she had done something wrong. Now Gertrude looked down her long nose at the messy tea table covered with bits of ribbon and paper. "And *where* shall I place the tray, Madam?" she asked Aunt Cornelia.

"Oh, anywhere will do," said Aunt Cornelia. She didn't look up. She was busy pasting cupids onto paper lace doilies.

Gertrude didn't move.

"Just put it on Samantha's stool by the fire, Gertrude," said Aunt Cornelia. "Sam can sit on the floor."

"The *floor*, Madam?" sniffed Gertrude.

"Yes," said Aunt Cornelia. "And Gertrude, would you mix up another batch of flour paste for us, please? We've used up this jar." She handed Gertrude the sticky jar of paste.

If Aunt Cornelia had handed her a pail of snakes and hoptoads, Gertrude could not have looked more disgusted. She held the paste jar with the very tips of her fingers as she left the room.

Aunt Cornelia brought Samantha a cup of sweet, hot tea and looked down at the valentine Samantha had just finished. "Oh, how lovely!" she exclaimed. "Grandmary and the Admiral will love it!"

"Oh, how lovely!" Aunt Cornelia exclaimed.
"Grandmary and the Admiral will love it!"

Samantha set the valentine carefully on a corner of the table. "Now I'll make one for Nellie," she said. "This one has to be especially pretty because Nellie is my very best friend in Mount Bedford."

"You miss her a lot, don't you?" said Aunt Cornelia.

"Yes," said Samantha. "And I worry about her, too. She has to work very hard at Mrs. Van Sicklen's, and she's not very strong."

Aunt Cornelia sighed. "But Nellie is better off there than she would be here in the city."

"I know," said Samantha. "When Nellie lived in the city before, she worked in a terrible, dangerous factory. It was horrible."

"At least Nellie had a loving family to go home to," said Aunt Cornelia. "Lots of children who work in those factories are orphans. The lucky ones live in orphanages. The others live on the streets."

Samantha shivered. She had seen many poor, raggedy children in the city. She was glad Nellie was safe with her family in Mount Bedford, even if she *was* far away. "Maybe we could make valentine cookies and send them to Nellie," said Samantha.

"What a good idea!" said Aunt Cornelia. "We'll make cookies for Nellie and Agnes and Agatha . . ."

"And Uncle Gard!" added Samantha. "It will be a surprise for him!"

"A surprise?" Uncle Gard poked just his head into the parlor. "Are my two best girls planning a surprise for me? Well, I've got a surprise, too," he said. He reached into the pocket of his coat and handed Samantha a postcard and a letter.

"Oooh, look!" said Samantha. "It's a postcard from Grandmary and the Admiral." She read aloud Grandmary's elegant, spidery script:

My dear Samantha,

The Admiral and I are sailing in the warm, blue-green waters off Greece. It's lovely! We're very happy, but we do miss our dear girl. Please give our love to your Uncle Gardner and Aunt Cornelia.

Ever your devoted,

Grandmary

Ahoy matey! What ho! xoxo your Admiral

Samantha laughed. "Look," she said. "The Admiral drew a picture for all of us." She handed the card to Uncle Gard and Aunt Cornelia and looked down at the letter in her lap. "Jiminy!" she exclaimed. "It's from Nellie!" She ripped open the envelope eagerly and began to read aloud:

"Dear Samantha, How are you? I hope you are very happy living at your Aunt and Uncle's house. I am fine, but . . ."

Suddenly, Samantha stopped reading aloud because the words were too horrible. She read to herself:

I am fine, but I have some very sad news. The flu has been very bad here in Mount Bedford this winter. We all had it except Jenny. My mother and father died. I miss them so much. Mrs. Van Sicklen says they are in heaven where God will take care of them. Mrs. Van Sicklen has been kind, but now we must leave her house. Bridget and Jenny

8

and I are moving to New York City to live with our Uncle Mike. I will come to see you as soon as I can. I promise.

Your friend,
Nellie

"Oh, poor Nellie!" Samantha whispered. "Poor Bridget and Jenny!"

"What is it, Samantha?" Aunt Cornelia asked.

Samantha couldn't talk. She was too afraid she would cry. She handed the letter to Aunt Cornelia.

Aunt Cornelia and Uncle Gard read it together. When they finished, Uncle Gard picked Samantha up and held her in his lap. Aunt Cornelia took both her hands.

"Sometimes," Aunt Cornelia said in a soft, slow voice, "sometimes it's very hard to understand why such sad, sad things happen to good people, people we love. Nellie and her sisters are very young to be without their parents. But they have their uncle, and I am sure he will take care of them."

Uncle Gard cleared his throat. Samantha knew

he and Aunt Cornelia were both just as sad as she was. "Nellie and her little sisters will be in New York, Sam. They won't be far away anymore," he said. "We'll be able to see them and be sure they're all right. Isn't that so, Cornelia?"

Aunt Cornelia didn't answer, but she squeezed Samantha's hands.

"Nellie says she'll come to see me when she gets to New York," Samantha said. It was the one good thing in the middle of the sadness—like one candle in a big, dark room. "Nellie promised to come, so I know she will. Oh, I hope she comes soon!"

CHAPTER
TWO

—

SEARCHING FOR NELLIE

Days and days went by, but Nellie never came. There was no note, no message, no word at all from her. Every afternoon Samantha hurried home from school and sat, waiting, in the front parlor. She pretended to do her schoolwork, but really she stared out the window, hoping to see Nellie coming toward her. But she saw only strangers.

Her hopes faded as each bright afternoon faded into gray twilight. She read Nellie's letter over and over again, adding up the days in her head. One day for Nellie to pack, one day to travel, one day with her uncle . . .

Samantha began to worry. Maybe something

11

had happened. Maybe Nellie was sick with the flu again. Maybe Mrs. Van Sicklen wanted her to stay in Mount Bedford. Or maybe her uncle wouldn't let her come to visit. Something had to be wrong, because if Nellie was in New York, Samantha knew that she would keep her promise.

The first few evenings, as soon as Uncle Gard came in the door, he asked about Nellie. "Did she come today, Sam?" But after a while, he didn't need to ask. He could tell the answer was no by the disappointed look on Samantha's face.

One night after dinner, Uncle Gard said, "Tonight we'll telephone Mrs. Van Sicklen and find out where Nellie and her sisters are."

"That's a good idea," said Aunt Cornelia.

"Telephone?" asked Samantha. "But it's all the way to Mount Bedford. That's long distance."

"Well, what else do we have a newfangled contraption like the telephone for?" asked Uncle Gard.

Samantha and Aunt Cornelia followed Uncle Gard into the hallway and watched as he cranked the telephone. "Operator?" he shouted into the mouthpiece.

"Hello? Operator? I want to speak to the Van
Sicklen residence in Mount Bedford, please."
Samantha heard some loud crackling on the line,
then Uncle Gard shouted, "Mrs. Van Sicklen,
please. Mrs. Van Sicklen? Gardner Edwards here.
No, no, nothing's wrong. Sorry to alarm you by
telephoning. We're wondering where Nellie is.
Nellie, your little maid, and her sisters Bridget
and Jenny."

Uncle Gard paused. Then his voice was serious.
"Two weeks ago? I see. Well, do you happen to
know their uncle's exact address? No? I don't
suppose he has a telephone? No, no, I thought not.
Well, thank you, Mrs. Van Sicklen. I'll ring off
now." He turned the crank, hung up the earpiece,
then looked at Samantha.

"Mrs. Van Sicklen says the girls left Mount
Bedford two weeks ago. She put them on the train
herself. The uncle's name is Mike O'Malley. Mrs.
Van Sicklen didn't know his exact address, but she
thinks he lives somewhere near the river, on 17th
or 18th Street."

"They left Mount Bedford two weeks ago,"
repeated Samantha. "Why hasn't Nellie come to see

me in all that time?"

"Nellie may be working," Uncle Gard said. "Or maybe she's too busy looking after Bridget and Jenny."

Samantha felt desperate. "Can't we try to find them? If we could just find where Nellie's uncle lives—"

"Samantha," Aunt Cornelia interrupted gently, "New York is a big place. It would be very hard—probably impossible—to find Nellie's uncle by just wandering around. I'm afraid all we can do is wait for Nellie to come to us."

"Don't give up hope, Sam," said Uncle Gard. "Nellie will come one of these days. I'm sure she will."

He tried to turn his worried frown into a smile, but Samantha could tell by his voice that Uncle Gard wasn't really sure Nellie *would* come. Samantha was quiet for a moment. She was thinking hard. Then she said, "Thank you for telephoning, Uncle Gard." She climbed up the stairs to her room. With each step, she was more determined. She didn't care how hard it would be. She was going to find Nellie. And she would go the very next day.

After school the next afternoon, Samantha set off under the heavy gray sky. She was more than a little nervous. In just a few blocks, she was in a part of the city she had never seen before. But she followed the street signs carefully and found 17th Street without any trouble. A strong wind at her back seemed to push her right to it.

But after she had walked toward the river for five or six blocks, 17th Street changed. Samantha had to jostle her way down the icy, muddy middle of the street because the sidewalks were blocked with pushcarts. The carts were piled high with potatoes, baskets, brooms, and buckets. The air was so full of the smell of fish and smoke, it seemed as dense as fog.

And there were so many people! Women dressed all in black with shawls over their heads poked at the things on the carts. Silent men stood next to small fires, rubbing their hands. Packs of raggedy-looking boys ran through the crowd.

Samantha began to feel as small and timid as a mouse in the hubbub around her. All the noise and strangeness was frightening. But she could not turn back. *It's a good thing there are so many people out on the street,* she said to herself bravely. *Someone here must know Nellie's uncle.*

But the cold that was chilling her hands and feet seemed to be freezing up her courage, too. When she saw steam rising from a cart of roasted chestnuts, she decided to get some because they looked so nice and hot.

Samantha handed the chestnut man a penny. As he gave her the bag of nuts, he said, "There you are, missy. The chestnuts will cheer ye. Put 'em in your muff to warm up your hands."

His singsong accent reminded Samantha of the way Nellie's father had talked. "Please, sir," she said. "Do you know Mr. O'Malley?"

The man grinned. "Sure and there are many, many O'Malleys, miss. Which one would you be wanting?"

"Mr. Mike O'Malley," said Samantha. "He lives on 17th or 18th Street."

The grin vanished from the man's face like a light blown out by a cold wind. "And what would a young missy such as yourself be wanting with a

hooligan like Mike O'Malley?" he asked.

"My friend Nellie, his niece, is with him," said Samantha. "Please, do you know where he lives?"

The man thought for a moment, then he said, "Last I heard he was living—if you can call it that—over on 18th Street, above the shoemaker."

"Thank you!" said Samantha.

"Mind you be careful!" warned the chestnut man as Samantha hurried away.

She walked fast, but she was worried. Was Nellie's uncle a bad man? The chestnut man had called him a hooligan. Samantha was not sure what a hooligan was, but she was quite sure she did not want to meet one. Only the idea of finally seeing Nellie kept her going. By now she was expert at dodging people and carts. In no time she'd rounded the corner and found the shoemaker's shop on 18th Street. There, outside the shop, she stopped. She stood silently staring at the building.

Is this where Nellie lives? she wondered. The building was gloomy and horrible. It was falling apart and looked as if it were too tired to stand up anymore. Tattered laundry hung from the windows like grimy flags of defeat.

Samantha did not want to go in the dark doorway. Then she thought, *Maybe Nellie has to go in this doorway every single day. Maybe Nellie is inside there right now.*

She climbed the steps and went inside. The door slammed shut behind her as if the building were swallowing her whole. The hallway smelled like rotting garbage. It was so dark, Samantha could hardly see. She held her breath and started up the creaky steps. Suddenly, at the top of the steps, a door flew open and a woman stuck her head out.

18

"What do you want?" she asked in a hard voice.

Samantha froze. "I'm . . . uh, I'm looking for Mr. Mike O'Malley," she croaked.

"Hist!" frowned the woman. "You'll not find him here, I'm happy to say. Now go away!" She started to close the door.

"Please, ma'am," said Samantha. "I was told he lived here. I've got to find him. He's got Nellie, and . . ."

"Nellie?" asked the woman. She stopped closing the door. A little face appeared at her knees, peeking around her skirts, smiling at Samantha. The woman scooped up the baby and opened the door a bit wider. "Is it Nellie you're looking for?"

"Yes!" said Samantha.

The woman still didn't smile, but she said, "Come along in then! Quickly now!"

Samantha stepped inside. She stood awkwardly near the door in a small room. It was not much lighter than the hallway, but it was scrubbed clean. It was more crowded than any room Samantha had ever seen. It was everything at once. One part was a kitchen. There were beds, and chairs pushed together to make beds, in each corner. In the middle of the room there was a wooden table where six children sat. They were making flowers out of paper. They all looked up shyly at Samantha, but their fingers never stopped twisting the colorful paper onto wire stems. It seemed odd to see the bright blossoms in the middle of the dark, cheerless room.

"All right, children," said the woman kindly. "Gawking won't get the work done faster, will it?" She bounced the baby on her hip while she told her story. "That Mike O'Malley," she said, as if the name were a curse. "He did live here, and drinking was all he was good for, you'll pardon me saying, miss. Then about two weeks ago, the three girls came to live with him. Good, polite girls they were, too. And if Mike O'Malley didn't take all of their money and anything else they had, and run off! He left them all alone in that room upstairs. They had nothing to eat and nowhere to sleep but the bare floor. Well! The oldest one, that Nellie, was as bright a child as I've ever seen. She tried to clean up the place and make it decent, but they couldn't stay there with no coal for a fire and not two pennies to rub together. So I took them in here.

"But we're crowded in here already, as you can see," the woman said.
"So I had to take Nellie and her sisters to the orphanage."

21

They sat down to work, and there was never a word of complaint from one of them. But we're crowded in here already, as you can see. After about a week, Nellie said they couldn't stay and be eating our food any longer. So I did the only thing I knew to do. I took them to the orphanage, where at least they'll be safe and warm and fed and get some schooling. Aye, and didn't it break my heart to see them go."

"They're gone?" asked Samantha. "To an orphanage?"

"Yes," said the woman. "Over on 20th Street. It's called Coldrock House for Homeless Girls." She shook her head. "They've got no one left in the world to care for them now, poor things. Though you mark my words, they're better off without that good-for-nothing uncle."

Samantha couldn't believe what she had heard. Nellie and the girls were in an orphanage! Coldrock House didn't sound very warm or welcoming, but it had to be better than living with their Uncle Mike. "Thank you," Samantha said to the woman. "Now I know where to find Nellie. Thank you for being so kind."

"It's the least I could do for the dear girls," said the woman. "If you see Nellie and the little ones, give them my best love and say I still think of them and wish I could do more for them myself."

Samantha shook the woman's hand. "I will," she said. "I'll tell them."

Then she turned and rushed down the steps, out into the steely-gray dusk. She hurried home through the shadowy streets, thinking only of Nellie and her sisters.

CHAPTER
THREE
—

COLDROCK HOUSE

Samantha couldn't sleep that night. She pulled the blankets up to her nose, but above them her eyes were wide open. She listened to the swoosh and sigh of the sleet against her window. She heard the passing horses snort and stamp and jingle their harnesses to shake off the dreary cold. Mostly, she worried about Nellie. What kind of place was Coldrock House for Homeless Girls? Was Nellie all right there? Tomorrow she would see for herself.

The next morning at breakfast, Aunt Cornelia said, "You look tired, Samantha. Do you feel all right?"

"Oh yes, I'm fine," said Samantha. "I just . . .

24

I just didn't sleep too much last night."

Uncle Gard's face wrinkled with concern. "Now, Sam," he said, "I know you're worried about Nellie and the little ones. I am, too. It's hard not really knowing how they are, or even exactly where they are."

"I do know exactly where they are," Samantha said quietly.

"You do?" asked Uncle Gard and Aunt Cornelia together.

Samantha nodded. "Nellie and Bridget and Jenny are in an orphanage. It's called Coldrock House for Homeless Girls. It's on 20th Street."

Uncle Gard and Aunt Cornelia were silent.

"I know because I went to Nellie's uncle's house yesterday," Samantha went on. "And a neighbor told me about Nellie."

Uncle Gard and Aunt Cornelia looked at each other. Then Uncle Gard said, "Samantha, you went to a dangerous part of the city. Don't go there again. Do you understand?"

"Yes," said Samantha. "I'm sorry. I just had to try to find Nellie and the girls. And now I know where they are. At Coldrock House."

"I'll go to Coldrock House with you this afternoon," said Aunt Cornelia. "They might not allow you in if you're by yourself."

"Thank you!" said Samantha. She smiled for the first time that morning.

Aunt Cornelia smiled back. "We'll *VALISE* pack a small valise for Nellie and her sisters," she said. "I'm sure they could use some warm clothes."

"Yes! And books," said Samantha. "Nellie loves books, and pens and paper and . . ."

"Cookies!" exclaimed Uncle Gard. "And sweets!"

Samantha laughed. "You're right, Uncle Gard," she said as she hugged him. She knew he was relieved to know where Nellie and her sisters were, too.

It was biting cold that afternoon when Samantha and Aunt Cornelia walked to Coldrock House. Samantha followed her aunt up the steps to the stern, unwelcoming building. The building looked as if it had been built out of blocks of dirty gray ice. It was surrounded by a fence of sharp black spikes. Samantha couldn't tell if the spikes were meant to keep visitors *out* or the orphans *in*.

A pale, pinched-looking maid opened the door when Aunt Cornelia knocked. "Would you announce me to the directress?" Aunt Cornelia said. "I'm Cornelia Edwards, and this is my niece Samantha Parkington."

Without a word, the maid led them to a dark, cold parlor. It was very, very quiet. Samantha couldn't believe the building had children in it. Didn't any of them make a noise?

Suddenly, soundlessly, a stout woman appeared. She was frowning. When she saw Aunt Cornelia and Samantha, her eyes narrowed for a moment. She studied her two well-dressed guests, and then she smiled a fake smile. Her eyes widened with put-on delight. "How perfectly lovely," she exclaimed, holding her hand out to Aunt Cornelia. "Mrs. Edwards! Miss Parkington! How nice of you to visit us! I'm Tusnelda Frouchy, the directress here at Coldrock House. Please sit down. And how may I help you? Have you come to hire a maid or a serving girl?"

"Not today," replied Aunt Cornelia. "We've come to see Nellie O'Malley."

Miss Frouchy looked surprised. Her sickly-sweet

smile faltered for a moment, then spread itself wide again. "That's impossible," she said. "Our girls have visitors on Sunday afternoons only, from three to four o'clock. That's the rule. I'm sorry." She didn't sound sorry at all.

"This is a special case," Aunt Cornelia said firmly. "Nellie is a dear friend of my niece's. We haven't seen her in a long time. I'm sure you understand."

Miss Frouchy patted Samantha's cheek. Her puffy hands were soft but very, very cold. Samantha did not think she liked Miss Tusnelda Frouchy.

"I had no idea Nellie had such perfectly lovely friends," Miss Frouchy said. She turned to the maid and snapped, "Get her." While they waited, Miss Frouchy went on. "Nellie and her sisters are new here at Coldrock House, and of course, they're still a bit . . . a bit independent-minded, shall we say. But they'll adjust, I'm sure. Our girls quickly learn the rules here: Obedience. Order. Discipline . . ."

"Nellie!" cried Samantha. She jumped out of her chair and ran to hug her friend. "Nellie! I'm so glad to see you!"

 "Samantha?" Nellie didn't seem to believe her eyes. "Oh, Samantha! You're here!" Nellie's face was full of joy.

"I was so worried when you didn't come to Uncle Gard and Aunt Cornelia's," said Samantha. "I even went to your uncle's house to find you and Bridget and Jenny."

"You didn't!" gasped Nellie. Her eyes were wide. "How did you ever—"

"Nellie!" Miss Frouchy interrupted. Her voice was very sharp.

Samantha felt Nellie stiffen. "Yes, Miss Frouchy," Nellie said.

"We haven't forgotten our manners, have we? Say 'how do you do' to Mrs. Edwards." Miss Frouchy turned to Aunt Cornelia. "You'll have to forgive her." She sighed. "Good manners are an important part of Coldrock House training, but these rough girls come to us without any idea of polite behavior at all." She held up her hands helplessly.

Now Samantha was sure she didn't like Miss Frouchy. Imagine calling Nellie rough! She could feel her face grow red with anger. But she bit her tongue as Nellie curtsied and murmured, "How do you do, Mrs. Edwards."

"Nellie," Aunt Cornelia said kindly, "we're so sorry about your parents—"

"Such a sad thing!" interrupted Miss Frouchy. She shook her head and pursed her lips, pretending to feel sympathy.

"Do you and Bridget and Jenny need anything?" Aunt Cornelia asked Nellie.

Before Nellie could answer, Miss Frouchy exclaimed, "Oh, nothing at all! They have warm clothes, good food, and a roof over their heads. They're learning how to make their way in the world as servants. But most important of all, they're learning to be grateful to their betters and to be obedient, hard-working girls." She turned to Nellie and asked, "Isn't that so, Nellie?"

"Yes, Miss Frouchy, ma'am," said Nellie, looking down at the floor.

Samantha studied Nellie while Miss Frouchy made a long speech about what a fine place the orphanage was. Nellie's hair was chopped short. Her drab brown dress was much too big. It was

*"But most important of all, they're learning to be grateful to their
betters. Isn't that so, Nellie?" Miss Frouchy said.*

made out of scratchy material as rough as a potato sack. Nellie looked smaller and thinner than ever. Miss Frouchy said she was getting good food, but Samantha could see she definitely wasn't getting *enough* of it.

"Nellie," she said in a quiet voice, hoping Miss Frouchy wouldn't hear. "Look. We brought some things for you and Bridget and Jenny. We brought books and clothes and socks." Samantha began to unpack the valise. "We even brought some gingerbread, and . . ."

Suddenly, Miss Frouchy pounced like a tiger and snatched the things away. "I'll keep these for Nellie," she said. "We don't want the girls eating too much rich food. It's not good for them. And we don't want to spoil them with gifts. It makes them selfish. Isn't that right, Nellie?"

Nellie looked at Samantha helplessly.

"Isn't that right, Nellie?" Miss Frouchy hissed. Her green eyes were narrowed.

"Yes, Miss Frouchy, ma'am," Nellie answered in a whisper.

Samantha didn't know what to do. She couldn't

talk to Nellie with Miss Frouchy there. Luckily, Aunt Cornelia understood. "Miss Frouchy," she said, "would you be kind enough to give me a tour of Coldrock House? I'm so interested in your work here."

Miss Frouchy seemed to puff up with pleasure and pride. "Why, of course," she said. "Do come with me."

Aunt Cornelia smiled and winked at the girls as she followed Miss Frouchy from the room.

"Jiminy! That Miss Frouchy is terrible!" exclaimed Samantha when she and Nellie were alone. "I just know she'll eat that gingerbread all by herself."

Nellie grinned, and suddenly she looked like her old self.

"Oh, Nellie," Samantha said. "Are you really, really all right?"

"It's not so bad here," said Nellie. "At least we're together. That's the most important thing of all."

"Are Bridget and Jenny all right?" asked Samantha.

Nellie's grin faded. "Well, Bridget's not strong,

and Miss Frouchy thinks she's lazy and scolds her terribly. I try to do Bridget's work for her, but it's hard to fool Miss Frouchy. She's everywhere! She's as sneaky as a cat."

Samantha squinted her eyes and made a catty face like Miss Frouchy's. "Perfectly lovely!" she mimicked.

Nellie tried to hide her giggles behind her hand.

Samantha sighed. "I wish you three could come to live with Uncle Gard and Aunt Cornelia and me," she said.

"No," said Nellie. "They've got all the maids they need. They don't want us."

"Well then you could run away from here and *hide* at Uncle Gard and Aunt Cornelia's!" said Samantha. "They'd never know. You could stay in the attic, and I could take care of you and bring you food and everything—"

"Samantha," interrupted Nellie, "you know that would never work. If we ran away, we'd be caught and punished—really punished." Nellie looked very serious. "The best thing we can do is to stay here. They're training me to be a maid. Pretty soon they'll find a job for me, and I'll be able to

34

work and take care of Bridget and Jenny."

"But—" Samantha began.

"Don't you see?" said Nellie. "All we've got is one another. Bridget and Jenny and I *have* to stay together. That's all that matters."

Samantha knew she could not change Nellie's mind. "Can you at least come visit Uncle Gard and Aunt Cornelia and me?"

"No," said Nellie. "Miss Frouchy wouldn't let us. But you can visit us here on Sundays."

"Only for an hour, and with that grouchy Miss Frouchy watching us," said Samantha. "Oh, well," she sighed. "It's better than nothing. And I can bring you things, lots of things, like—" Just then Miss Frouchy came back into the room, so the girls had to stop talking. She hardly let them say good-bye before she sent Nellie away.

Aunt Cornelia was very quiet on the walk home. Samantha could tell she had not liked what she had seen of Coldrock House. All she said was, "Those poor children." She shook her head and put her arm around Samantha's shoulder to hold her close by her side.

35

RUNAWAYS!

Uncle Gard, Aunt Cornelia, and
Samantha were waiting outside
Coldrock House at exactly five minutes
before three o'clock the next Sunday afternoon.
They didn't want to miss a second of their visiting
hour with Nellie, Bridget, and Jenny. They were all
quite cheerful when they arrived, but they left
feeling sad.

All the way home, Uncle Gard fussed and
fumed about the way Miss Frouchy treated the
girls. He had spent the hour talking to Bridget and
Jenny. He had kept a serious expression on his face,
hoping to fool Miss Frouchy into thinking he was
quizzing the girls on the multiplication tables. But

really he was asking them, "Miss Bridget O'Malley, where did you get those wonderful curls?" and "Miss Jenny O'Malley, how did you make your eyes such a pretty blue?" Bridget and Jenny tried to answer him just as seriously, but once in a while they'd break out into giggles. Whenever they did, they looked nervously at Miss Frouchy. She would narrow her eyes and frown at them. And when Uncle Gard tried to give them some sweets, Miss Frouchy grabbed them away.

Samantha and Nellie talked as much and as fast as they could, but one hour was nowhere near enough time. At the end of the visit, Samantha asked Nellie in a whisper, "Can't we meet secretly? What if I sneak over here in the middle of the night when everyone is asleep? I can tap on your window, and you can climb out."

Nellie laughed. "I have a better idea. What if you came in the afternoon, on your way home from school? It's my job to empty the ashes from the fireplaces. I bring them to the ash cans in the alley out back every afternoon about four o'clock. Could you come then?"

"Oh, of course!" said Samantha.

So every afternoon after school, Samantha hurried off to visit Nellie at Coldrock House. Samantha had to be very careful to get there by four o'clock. If she was even five minutes late, she didn't see Nellie at all.

Even though they met almost every afternoon, it never seemed that the girls had enough time together. While they talked, Samantha emptied the ashes into the cans so that Nellie had time to eat the food Samantha brought her. Nellie always looked hungry and tired and pale. Samantha noticed her friend's hands were red and chapped from the cold, so she gave Nellie her gloves. But the next afternoon, Nellie wasn't wearing them.

"Why aren't you wearing the gloves?" Samantha asked.

Nellie looked sorry. "Miss Frouchy took them," she said.

"That old cat!" exclaimed Samantha. "Didn't you tell her they were yours?"

"Yes," said Nellie, "but when I wouldn't tell her where I got them, she said I must have stolen them."

"Stolen them!" sputtered Samantha. "*She* stole

them from *you!* I'd like to march right inside and take those gloves away from Miss Tusnelda Frouchy."

"Samantha, don't," Nellie warned. "If Miss Frouchy knew we were meeting, she'd be awfully mad. She'd—"

"Punish you?" Samantha finished for her.

Nellie nodded.

"Did she punish you for the gloves?" Samantha asked.

Nellie nodded again. "No dinner," she said.

Samantha frowned. "From now on I'll bring more food instead of things like gloves. You can eat it right away or give it to Bridget and Jenny."

"That would be much better," said Nellie.

"I'll bring as much food as I can sneak past Gertrude," Samantha promised. "She's our stingy housekeeper. She's already noticed I seem to need more food than I ever did before. It won't be easy, so don't you let fat old Miss Frouchy get any of it!"

"Don't worry," grinned Nellie. "We'll eat it so fast she'll never get a whiff of it!"

❧

As the days went by, the afternoons seemed to be getting softer. The sun was still as pale as a pearl, but every day more light and warmth found its way to the narrow alley behind Coldrock House where Nellie and Samantha met. Then one afternoon Nellie seemed much quieter than usual. She hardly seemed to hear Samantha's questions, and she put the apples Samantha brought in her apron pocket without even looking at them.

"What's the matter, Nellie?" Samantha asked at last. "Has Miss Frouchy been punishing you again?"

"No," said Nellie.

"Then what?" asked Samantha.

Nellie slammed the lid onto the ash can so loudly it made Samantha jump. "They've picked me to go on the Orphan Train," said Nellie.

"What's *that?*" asked Samantha.

"It's a train that goes out West. It's full of orphans from the city. The train stops in lots of little farm towns. People in the towns choose orphans to live with them and to work for them," Nellie explained.

Samantha was horrified. "But Nellie, you *can't*

*"They've picked me to go out West
on the Orphan Train," said Nellie.*

leave New York!"

"I don't have any choice," Nellie said. "Miss Frouchy says I have to go. I'm trained enough now, and I'm old enough to work. Farm people might want me."

"What about Bridget and Jenny?" Samantha asked.

"They're too young to go," Nellie said softly. "They'll stay here."

"Oh, no," said Samantha. "You'll be separated."

"Yes," said Nellie. Her eyes filled with tears.

"Nellie, we can't let that happen," Samantha said. "You and Bridget and Jenny may never see one another again." She looked Nellie square in the eyes. "Now you've *got* to run away. You've *got* to come to Uncle Gard and Aunt Cornelia's house and hide. Just for a while, just until we think of something else to do. Please, Nellie, please say you'll come."

Nellie thought for a moment. "If I could look for work while I was there . . ."

"Oh, yes!" said Samantha. "You can go out every morning and come back in at night. No one will see you. I'll be sure of that. And I'll be sure you have food and blankets and everything you need."

Nellie sighed. "It's not a very practical plan," she said. "It won't work for long, but it's our only choice."

"Then you'll do it?" asked Samantha.

Nellie smiled a little smile. "I guess so," she said. "We might as well try."

Samantha hugged Nellie hard. "Good!" she said. "Bring Bridget and Jenny with you tomorrow afternoon at four."

"All right," said Nellie. "I'll find a way."

"Don't worry," said Samantha. "I'll plan everything. You'll see, Nellie. It will be fine. This will be your last night at Coldrock House."

"I hope so," said Nellie. "I certainly hope so."

≈

The next day after school, Samantha ran to Coldrock House so fast she was there way too early. She waited next to the ash cans, hopping from one foot to the other, filled with nervous jitters. When the loud bell rang at four o'clock on the dot, Samantha stood perfectly still. It felt like forever, but it was really only a minute or two before Nellie, Jenny, and Bridget appeared. The two little girls looked so confused and fearful, Samantha tried to calm them.

"Everything will be all right," she said. "Here. Put these on." Samantha handed Bridget and Jenny shawls and scarves she'd brought to cover up their orphan uniforms. "They're sort of disguises," she explained.

She and Nellie helped Bridget and Jenny wrap themselves up. Nellie grinned. "They're so bundled up they can hardly walk," she said. "So they certainly aren't runaways. They're more like waddle-aways."

Samantha smiled, but nervously. "All right," she said. "Let's go." She took Jenny's cold little hand in her own, and Nellie took Bridget's. The four girls walked in a tunnel of sunshine down the alley to the street, leaving Coldrock House behind them.

No one paid any attention to them as they walked the few blocks to Uncle Gard and Aunt Cornelia's house. Jenny trotted along next to

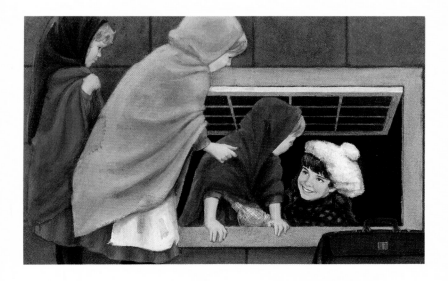

Samantha trustfully. It made Samantha feel very grown-up—like a big sister—to have Jenny relying on her so completely. She held Jenny's hand very tightly.

Samantha led the way to the alley behind the house. "We'll have to climb in this window to the basement storage room," she explained in a soft voice. "The back stairs start in the basement and go all the way up to the top floor. When we get inside, we'll take our shoes off so no one will hear us. There's a door that leads to the kitchen right off the stairs, so be very quiet when we pass it. Gertrude may be in the kitchen. She notices everything and she's kind of mean, so just follow me and don't talk. Ready?"

Nellie, Jenny, and Bridget nodded. Samantha climbed through the small window into the dark basement, then reached up to help Jenny through. When they were all inside, Samantha tiptoed to the stairs and started up. There was a lot of noise in the kitchen. Gertrude seemed to be banging pots and pans together, and the laundry wringer was going thump, thump, thump.

As quietly as whispers, the four girls climbed the steps up to the main floor, up past the bedroom floor, and up to the very top floor. Samantha put her finger to her lips and slowly, slowly opened the door at the top of the stairs. She peeked her head out and looked around. No one was there. She motioned the three girls to follow her, and they quickly darted into the empty room across the hall.

They all sighed with relief. "Phew!" said Samantha. "I've been holding my breath ever since we climbed in the window. I was about to burst!"

"Me, too!" said Nellie. She looked around the room. Winter sunshine made bright yellow patches

of warmth on the thin, faded rug.
Samantha had brought up lots of
her books and toys to make the
room look welcoming and homey.
Jenny and Bridget sat right down
and started to play with Saman-
tha's pretty paper dolls. Nellie smiled when she saw
the blackboard they used to have in the Mount
Better School. "Everything looks very nice," she
said to Samantha. "Thank you."

"It's a little cold up here," said Samantha. "I'm
sorry you can't have a fire. But I brought up all the
extra blankets I could find. Gertrude's room is right
down the hall. You'll have to be very quiet at night
and early in the morning while she's up here. I
hope you will be all right."

"We'll be fine," Nellie said cheerfully.

Jenny and Bridget were hungry, so Samantha
showed them the box of fruit and bread and cheese
she'd smuggled up to the room. They both took
apples to munch right away. "I couldn't bring very
much," Samantha explained. "Gertrude keeps an
eagle eye on the food in this house. But don't
worry. I'll find a way to bring more next time."

47

"Nellie," Jenny asked as she played with the paper dolls, "do we have to go back to Miss Frouchy at the orphanage tonight?"

"No," said Nellie. "We're going to stay here."

Jenny looked glad. "Does that mean we're not orphans anymore?"

"Well . . ." Nellie began.

Samantha knelt down and put her hand on Jenny's shoulder. "You and Bridget and Nellie are still together," she said. "And you'll never be orphans as long as you have one another."

"And good friends like Samantha," added Nellie with a smile.

TOGETHER

For the next few days, Samantha felt as if she lived in two different worlds. In one world, she made valentines and cookies with Aunt Cornelia. She went to school, practiced her ice skating, and joked with Uncle Gard, just as usual. The other world was smaller and quieter, but just as happy. That world was hidden away upstairs, in the room where her secret family lived. Samantha was a very important member of that family. It was up to her to be sure that Nellie, Bridget, and Jenny had food to eat, water for drinking and washing, books to read . . . everything they needed.

Every morning before dawn, Nellie crept down

the back stairs, climbed out the cellar window, and went about the city looking for work. She was gone all day. Bridget and Jenny stayed in the attic, playing with paper dolls, napping, and whispering quietly together. After their horrible days with their uncle and at the orphanage, they were happy to stay safe and cozy in their secret hideaway. And Nellie was always glad to get back to them at the end of the day.

Samantha loved being with Nellie again, and she liked being a big sister to Bridget and Jenny. Whenever she could manage it, she slipped away to be upstairs with her secret sisters. It was easy for Samantha to keep them happy and amused. They all loved to hear her tell about Aunt Cornelia and Uncle Gard. They asked hundreds of questions. What color dress was Aunt Cornelia wearing today? What did Uncle Gard say when Samantha got an "A" on a spelling test? Did Aunt Cornelia finish the valentines she was making? What did they look like? When were Aunt Cornelia and Samantha going to give Uncle Gard his valentine? The three girls listened to everything Samantha said with glowing eyes.

"Well," said Jenny one day, "I think your Aunt Cornelia and Uncle Gard are the finest lady and gentleman in New York City!"

"Yes!" agreed Bridget. "The only thing I liked at Coldrock House was when they visited. Once your Uncle Gard gave me a peppermint and Miss Frouchy didn't see," she remembered. "I made that peppermint last a long, long time. I wish I could have another one *right now.*"

"I wish you could, too," sighed Samantha.

She was having a hard time finding enough food for the hungry girls. Samantha gave them most of her lunch, all of her afternoon snack, and anything else she could smuggle from the pantry. One day she bought bread at the bakery and hurried home with the loaf hidden under her plaid cape. Another day she tried to bring a pot of cocoa to the girls. Bridget was catching a cold, and Samantha wanted her to have something warm to drink. But Gertrude stopped her at the kitchen door.

"Where are you going with that pot of cocoa?" Gertrude asked sharply.

"Up—upstairs," said Samantha.

51

"I won't have chocolate spilled all over your bedroom," said Gertrude. "Sit here at the kitchen table and drink it. Though I do not understand why you need to drink a whole pot of cocoa," she scolded. "I've never seen a child eat and drink as much as you have lately. Glass after glass of milk! Tea cakes and sandwiches all the live-long day! All the fruit from the bowl in the dining room! The way food disappears in this house, you'd think we had ten children living here instead of just one."

Samantha gulped her cocoa. Gertrude was getting suspicious!

So the next evening, when Samantha sneaked into the pantry, she tried to be very, very careful. Quietly, she opened the cookie jar. Quietly, she took three of the heart-shaped cookies she and Aunt Cornelia had made. She wanted to have a little party for Nellie, Bridget, and Jenny because the next day was Valentine's Day. She put the cookies in her pocket, turned to go, and there was Gertrude!

Gertrude blocked the doorway, her hands on her hips. "Cookies?" she snapped. "You just had dinner!" She frowned at Samantha. "Are you keeping a pet in this house? Is there some animal up in the attic? Is that what you are feeding?"

"Oh, no!" said Samantha nervously.

"All week I've heard scratches and scurrying up there at night when I'm in bed," said Gertrude. "There's *something* up there. I don't know whether it's mice or thieves or ghosts, but I'll find out sooner than soon!"

Samantha hurried away with her cookies. *She* knew what Gertrude was hearing. She'd have to warn the girls—and fast.

As soon as she was out of Gertrude's sight, she ran up the stairs. "You're going to have to be quieter than ever," Samantha panted to Jenny and Bridget. "Gertrude said she hears noises. And Nellie, maybe you'd better not go in and out for a few days. I'm afraid she may catch you on the stairs."

Nellie agreed sadly. "I haven't had any luck finding work anyway," she said. "No one wants me for a maid. They think I don't look strong enough." She sounded discouraged. "I think I'll probably have to go back to the thread factory where I worked before we moved to Mount Bedford."

"Don't give up yet, Nellie," said Samantha. "It's only been a few days."

"I know," said Nellie. "But we can't stay here forever."

Samantha knew Nellie was right. But she didn't know what to do.

Then, suddenly, the door flew open and Gertrude stormed in! "Whatever is going on here?" she demanded. "Who are these children? What are they doing here? What have you been up to, Miss Samantha?"

Samantha couldn't think of anything at all to say. She just sat there miserably.

"Well!" said Gertrude with a smirk. "I think you'd better come with me. And these ragamuffins had better come, too. Just wait till your aunt and uncle see this! You certainly have some explaining to do, young lady! Now get downstairs."

Gertrude crossed her arms on her chest and glared at the girls as they filed slowly past her and down the stairs. Samantha's heart sank with every step she took. Her plan had failed. Now the girls would have to go back to Coldrock House. They'd

"Whatever is going on here?" Gertrude demanded.
"Who are these children? What are they doing here?"

55

have to face Miss Frouchy and punishment for running away. Worse than that, now they would be separated. Probably forever. Nellie would be sent away on the Orphan Train.

Gertrude followed the girls into the parlor where Uncle Gard and Aunt Cornelia were sitting by the fire. When they saw Nellie and her sisters, they both gasped. "Why, Nellie! Bridget, Jenny! What are you doing here?" asked Aunt Cornelia.

"Begging your pardon, Madam," said Gertrude, her eyes bright with self-importance. "These raga-muffins were hiding in your attic. Street children! No better than beggars! They've probably been sneaking through your house stealing from you!"

"That's not true!" burst out Saman-tha. "They'd never take anything!"

"Then who's been stealing all the food?" asked Gertrude.

"*I* have," said Samantha. She was so mad she was almost crying. "*I'm* the thief, not them!"

"Now let's calm down," said Uncle Gard. "Samantha, perhaps you can explain all this."

"Well," she began. But just then Bridget sneezed.

"First, you'd better come sit here and get warm,"

Aunt Cornelia said gently. The four girls sat on the floor in front of the fire.

Samantha began again. "It's my fault. Nellie didn't want to run away from the orphanage. But Miss Frouchy was going to send her away on the Orphan Train. Bridget and Jenny were too young to go, so they would have had to stay at Coldrock House. They would never have seen Nellie again. So I talked Nellie into coming here, just until she could find a job where they could all be together."

"How long have they been here?" asked Aunt Cornelia.

"About four days," said Samantha.

"Four days!" exclaimed Aunt Cornelia. "But how did they eat?"

"I brought them food," said Samantha. "Gertrude is wrong. They'd never steal."

"I know that's true," said Aunt Cornelia. Uncle Gard didn't say anything. He just stared at the four sad girls.

Aunt Cornelia looked at him. "Well, Gardner," she said. "This is a very serious matter. What do you think we should do with these girls?"

"Give them warm baths and put them to bed,"

said Uncle Gard firmly. "We can decide the rest in the morning."

And that is exactly what they did. That night, Nellie, Bridget, and Jenny slept in Samantha's room. *This is probably the last time we'll be together,* thought Samantha as she watched the girls sleeping. Their faces were pink and peaceful in the firelight.

Late into the night, Samantha heard low murmurs coming from Uncle Gard and Aunt Cornelia's room. She knew they were deciding what to do with Nellie and Bridget and Jenny. Would they send them back to Coldrock House? Would they let them stay for just a little while longer? Would they try to find Nellie's uncle? Finally, Samantha couldn't wonder or worry any longer. She fell asleep.

The next morning when the girls came downstairs, there were three more places set at the breakfast table. And at every place there was a big red heart trimmed with lace.

"Happy Valentine's Day, girls," said Aunt Cornelia.

"Happy Valentine's Day," they all replied.

"Let's have breakfast," Uncle Gard said cheerfully.

The four girls sat down. But before she could swallow a crumb, Samantha's curiosity made her burst out, "Uncle Gard, Aunt Cornelia, have you decided? What are you going to do about Nellie and Bridget and Jenny? Couldn't they please stay here? They wouldn't be any trouble, and they'd be a big help around the house. They've all been taught to be maids . . ."

"We don't need any more maids," said Aunt Cornelia.

Samantha's heart sank.

"But we do need more girls here," said Uncle Gard. "I'd say we need three more girls, in a variety of sizes: tiny, medium, and still not very big." He turned to Nellie. "Miss Nellie O'Malley, how would you and Bridget and Jenny like to stay here? You could be sisters to Samantha and daughters to Cornelia and me?"

Nellie looked very serious. "We would like it very, very much," she answered.

"Hurray!" shouted Samantha. She bounced out of her chair and ran to hug Aunt Cornelia, then Nellie, Bridget, and Jenny. Then all four girls hugged Uncle Gard and showered him with kisses.

"Well," smiled Uncle Gard, "what a lovely Valentine's Day this turned out to be! I have *five* of the sweetest valentines anyone could ever have. I must be the luckiest person in the world!"

Samantha laughed. "No, Uncle Gard," she said. "*I'm* the luckiest person in the world. At last, at last, I have a real family of my own!"

LOOKING
BACK
1904

A PEEK INTO
THE PAST

American families relaxed on Sunday afternoon drives.

Wherever turn-of-the-century Americans looked, they saw a changing world. Automobiles were taking the place of horses even on country roads. By the time Samantha was nineteen years old, the Ford Motor Company had built over a million cars—all of them black! A new car came off the assembly line every three minutes. Trains linked every corner of the country. They could travel from New York to California in just four days. Today, jet planes make that same trip in six hours, but there were no jets at the turn of the century. The airplane, that "crazy, dangerous, newfangled contraption" the Wright brothers flew

The Wright brothers' airplane didn't carry passengers.

62

New York was already a big city in 1906.

in 1903, wasn't really used for passengers until Samantha was forty years old!

Cities continued to grow bigger and bigger as Samantha grew up. Every day hundreds of young people left their homes on America's farms to look for city jobs. Thousands of immigrants poured into American cities from all over the world. When they first arrived, most immigrants could not speak English. Some people made fun of them and only let them work as servants or peddlers, or in city factories for long hours at low pay. Many immigrants had to live in crowded, run-down tenements and slums. But the immigrants still found opportunities in this country. They worked hard to learn a new language, get better jobs, and earn more money. Soon

In 1907, more immigrants than ever before came to America.

These farm girls took city jobs to earn money.

they enjoyed a good life in their new land and became proud and respected Americans.

As Samantha grew up, more and more Americans obeyed the laws that said all children—rich and poor, boys and girls— should go to school until they were sixteen. Education helped young women get jobs and earn money to take care of themselves.

Back in the days when Grandmary was young, it wasn't proper for young ladies to even talk about money, and they certainly couldn't think about earning it! They were expected to live at home with their families until they got married and had husbands to take care of them. But by the time Samantha was old enough to work, people's attitudes had begun to change. Women could get jobs in department stores or in offices as secretaries—a job that only men had held before! Many women became phone operators, since more and more homes and offices had telephones.

Women who had gone to college became teachers or worked in a new profession called social work. One

Women worked as secretaries and telephone operators.

of the most famous social workers was a woman named Jane Addams, who founded Hull House, a settlement house that helped immigrants in Chicago learn English and trained them for work.

Even though women could finally have jobs and earn their own money, it still wasn't proper for them

Jane Addams, who founded Hull House in 1889, worked there her entire life.

to live alone. So there were special women's hotels and boarding houses where America's "working girls" could live and be carefully *chaperoned*, or looked after.

Once a young woman like Samantha got married, she quit her job, moved to a home of her own, and began to raise a family. Her home, like most in America, would have many "modern" inventions. Even people who were not wealthy had electric lamps, running

Electricity made housework easier.

When Samantha grew up, mothers and daughters did housework together.

water, gas stoves, refrigerators, and washing machines. Samantha would have needed these new machines to make housework easier because it was hard to find people who wanted to be servants. The immigrants who had been Grandmary's and Cornelia's maids had gotten better jobs, so a woman like Samantha had to do many chores herself.

Since there were few servants willing to take care of elaborate clothes like women wore at the turn of the century, fashions began to change, too. New styles were simpler to take care of and easier to wear. Back

when Grandmary was a young woman, her long skirts and petticoats with layers of ruffles might have weighed as much as 25 pounds. Young women like Cornelia raised their hemlines a bit and

As a young woman, Grandmary would have worn a dress like this.

1894

66

stopped squeezing themselves into tight corsets that made it hard to move and even to breathe. By the time Samantha was a young woman, skirts were even shorter and clothing was even looser. These new

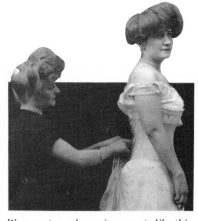

Women stopped wearing corsets like this.

styles upset some people. There were even laws that said women would have to pay a fine and go to jail if their skirts were more than three inches above the ankle!

But women liked the new freedom that shorter, more comfortable clothing gave them. These new styles seemed to be signs of the way women thought about themselves—as active people who had places to go and work to do. They were women who would not be hemmed in by old-fashioned clothing or old-fashioned attitudes.

| 1904 | 1909 | 1914 | 1919 | 1924 | 1929 |

As times changed, women shortened their dresses.